JIM PALMER
VERN STEPHENS
EDDIE MURRAY
CAL RIPKEN JR.
GUS TRIANDOS
MIKE MUSSINA
KEN SINGLETON
DAVE McNALLY
BROOKS ROBINSON
TONY BATISTA
FRANK ROBINSON
BRADY ANDERSON

THE HISTORY OF THE
BALTIMORE ORIOLES

JOHN NICHOLS

CREATIVE EDUCATION

Published by Creative Education, 123 South Broad Street, Mankato, MN 56001

Creative Education is an imprint of The Creative Company.

Designed by Rita Marshall.

Photographs by AllSport (Doug Pensinger, Matthew Stockman), Associated Press/Wide World Photos, Anthony Neste, Sports Gallery (Al Messerschmidt), SportsChrome (Greg Crisp, Rich Kane, Bryan Yablonsky), TimePix (Bob Gomel, Hank Walker)

Copyright © 2003 Creative Education. International copyright reserved in all countries. No part of this book may be reproduced in any form without written permission from the publisher.

Library of Congress Cataloging-in-Publication Data

Nichols, John, 1966- The history of the Baltimore Orioles / by John Nichols.

p. cm. — (Baseball)   ISBN 1-58341-201-8

Summary: Highlights the key personalities and memorable games in the history of the team that changed its name to the Orioles when it came to Baltimore from St. Louis in 1954.

1. Baltimore Orioles (Baseball team)—History—Juvenile literature. [1. Baltimore Orioles (Baseball team)—History.

2. Baseball—History.] I. Title. II. Baseball (Mankato, Minn.).

GV875.B2 N53 2002   796.357'64'097526—dc21   2001047859

First Edition 9 8 7 6 5 4 3 2 1

BALTIMORE,

MARYLAND, IS ONE OF AMERICA'S OLDEST AND MOST

culturally rich communities. Located on beautiful Chesapeake Bay, Baltimore is home to such historic sites as Fort McHenry, whose defense against the British in the War of 1812 inspired Francis Scott Key to write the words to America's national anthem. Baltimore has also had more than its share of famous citizens, including author Edgar Allen Poe and baseball great Babe Ruth.

Ruth may be Baltimore's most famous sports figure, but he is not the city's biggest connection to major league baseball. In 1954, the struggling St. Louis Browns franchise moved to Baltimore, hoping to turn around more than 50 years of losing baseball. Bought by a group of Baltimore businessmen, the franchise was renamed the Orioles and

GEORGE SISLER

dressed in orange and black in honor of the Maryland state bird.

{BASEBALL COMES TO BALTIMORE} The St. Louis Browns began playing in the American League (AL) in 1902. In its 52-year history, the team finished dead last 14 times and second-to-last 12 other seasons. Despite their poor record, the Browns did feature some great players, including first baseman George Sisler, pitcher Urban Shocker, and left fielder Ken Williams, all of whom starred in the 1920s. The Browns finally broke into the postseason in 1944, when star shortstop Vern Stephens led St. Louis to the AL pennant, but the Browns eventually lost the World Series to the crosstown St. Louis Cardinals.

After the World Series loss, the Browns went back to their losing ways for a decade. Then, before the 1954 season, team owner Bill Veeck sold the franchise, which became the Baltimore Orioles. The

In **1954**, the Orioles played 22 consecutive games on the road—a club record that still stands.

BRADY ANDERSON

Gene Woodling batted a team-high .300 in **1959** and made the AL All-Star team.

GENE WOODLING

first Orioles team fared no better than its Browns ancestors, finishing seventh in the eight-team AL. Despite the efforts of Stephens and such players as catcher Gus Triandos and outfielder Gene Woodling, things did not improve much throughout the 1950s. Still, Baltimore fans came out in droves to support their team.

With the money made from fan attendance, the team began to invest heavily in its minor-league system. Baltimore's plan was to develop young players by instilling a philosophy of solid fundamentals and a professional attitude. The plan came to be known as the "Oriole Way," a principle the team follows to this day. "There are no shortcuts to where we want to go," said Baltimore manager Paul Richards. "We plan to build this team from the ground up."

{ROBINSONS LEAD THE WAY} The first great player produced by the Oriole Way was a gangly third baseman named

Slugging catcher Gus Triandos provided much of Baltimore's offensive muscle in the **1950s**.

GUS TRIANDOS

Located in downtown Baltimore, Oriole Park at Camden Yards opened in **1992**.

ORIOLE PARK

Brooks Robinson. Brought to the majors for the first time as an 18-year-old in 1955, Robinson's weak bat kept him going back and forth between the Orioles and the minors for five straight years. Finally, Baltimore pitchers begged the team to keep Robinson with the big club because of his stellar defense. In 1960, Robinson stayed, and both he and the team had a breakthrough year. Led by rookie pitcher Chuck Estrada's league-leading 18 victories, shortstop Ron Hansen's 22 homers, and Robinson's .294 batting average and Gold Glove-winning play at third base, the Orioles posted their first winning season at 89–65.

The Orioles remained a contender for the next few years, but despite winning 90 or more games three times between 1961 and 1965, they could not capture a league title. Searching for the missing ingredient that would put the team over the top, Baltimore

*Brooks Robinson won the Gold Glove award for his defense every year from **1960** to **1975**.*

BROOKS ROBINSON

traded three players to the Cincinnati Reds for outfielder Frank Robinson. The 30-year-old Robinson had won the 1961 National League Most Valuable Player (MVP) award, but Reds management

decided he was "an old 30" and traded him. They couldn't have been more wrong.

In 1966, Frank Robinson led the league with a .316 average,

49 homers, and 122 RBI, capturing the Triple Crown (topping the league in all three categories). Meanwhile, Brooks Robinson added 23 homers and 100 RBI, and young pitchers Jim Palmer and Dave McNally anchored a talented pitching staff.

Behind these efforts, the Orioles soared to a pennant-winning 97–63 record. In the World Series, Baltimore faced the Los Angeles Dodgers. In game one, both Robinsons homered in a 5–2 Orioles victory. The favored Dodgers never recovered, and Baltimore rolled to a four-game sweep and its first world championship. "To do that to a ballclub as good as the Dodgers is almost unthinkable," exclaimed Brooks Robinson. "I'm just glad I was here to see it."

{FLYING HIGH UNDER WEAVER} Unfortunately, Baltimore was unable to maintain its championship ways. Midway through

*The Orioles dominated the Dodgers in the **1966** World Series, outscoring them 13–2 overall.*

JIM PALMER

the 1968 season, manager Hank Bauer was fired and replaced by Earl Weaver. The fiery new skipper had previously managed the organization's top minor-league team, and he quickly set about

lighting a fire under the Orioles.

In 1969, the Orioles were back with a vengeance, storming through the regular season with a club-record 109 victories. The team's offensive power again centered around the Robinsons but was helped considerably by the booming bat of burly first baseman Boog Powell and the speed of center fielder Paul Blair. The team's pitching staff also had a fine season, with Mike Cuellar winning 23 games and Palmer chipping in 16.

After cruising to the AL Eastern Division title (the league was divided into two divisions in 1969), Baltimore swept the Minnesota Twins in the AL Championship Series (ALCS) and faced the New York Mets in the World Series. The Orioles captured game one but then struggled, dropping the next four contests to lose the series.

Stung by their upset loss, the Orioles came out swinging in 1970. Baltimore went 108–54 to capture the AL East and then defeated Minnesota again in the ALCS to advance to the World

Lefty pitcher Dave McNally helped Baltimore capture world championships in **1966** and **1970**.

DAVE McNALLY

Like Brooks Robinson, **1990s** star Roberto Alomar was a superb defensive infielder.

Series. There, the Orioles faced the heavily favored Cincinnati Reds. Sparked by a dazzling series of fielding gems and big hits by Brooks Robinson, the Orioles stopped the "Big Red Machine" in five games. "Baseball is a team game, but what Brooks did is as close as I've ever seen one player come to winning a series by himself," said an amazed Earl Weaver.

> In his last season in Baltimore (**1971**), outfielder Frank Robinson cranked out 28 home runs.

In 1971, the Orioles' starting pitchers put together a season for the history books. McNally (21), Palmer (20), Cuellar (20), and Pat Dobson (20) became the first pitching staff since the 1920 Chicago White Sox to feature four 20-game winners. The Orioles also received solid contributions from slick-fielding shortstop Mark Belanger and outfielders Merv Rettenmund and Don Buford. These players led the Orioles back to the World Series, but Baltimore fell in seven games to the Pittsburgh Pirates.

FRANK ROBINSON

The Orioles continued their dominance through the mid-1970s, capturing division titles in 1973 and 1974. But by 1978, the team had changed dramatically. Frank Robinson was traded before

the 1972 season, Powell and McNally left the team in 1974, and Cuellar and Brooks Robinson were gone by 1977. The old stars had bid farewell. It was time for a new group to emerge.

{PITCHERS PAVE THE WAY} By 1979, a new generation of Orioles stars began to flex its muscles. Eddie Murray, the 1977 AL Rookie of the Year, was already among the best first basemen in the game. Speedy center fielder Al Bumbry was a base-stealing marvel, and third baseman Doug DeCinces and outfielder Ken Singleton provided abundant power. The team's pitching staff also was strong, led by three-time Cy Young Award winner Jim Palmer and young talents such as Mike Flanagan, Dennis Martinez, Scott McGregor, and reliever Tippy Martinez.

The rebuilt Orioles captured the AL East with a 102–57 mark in 1979. After defeating the California Angels in the ALCS, Baltimore faced the Pittsburgh Pirates in the World Series once again. Sadly, the result was also the same—the Orioles once again lost in seven games.

Al Bumbry swiped a team-leading 37 bases in **1979** and upped that number to 44 a year later.

AL BUMBRY

Infielder Eddie Murray was Baltimore's top RBI man every year from **1980** to **1986**.

EDDIE MURRAY

In 1982, Orioles fans saw one proud career come to an end while another was just beginning. That was the last year for manager Earl Weaver and the first for Cal Ripken Jr., Baltimore's new shortstop. Ripken—whose father was a longtime team coach—exploded onto the scene, hitting 28 home runs and driving in 93 runs to capture AL Rookie of the Year honors. The hardworking Ripken also proved durable, not missing a single game after May 29, beginning a streak of consecutive games played that would become his trademark.

In 1983, new manager Joe Altobelli guided the Orioles to a superb season. The team rolled to the AL East title, then defeated the Chicago White Sox for the pennant. In the World Series, Baltimore lost the opening game to the Philadelphia Phillies. But then the Orioles' powerful pitching took control as Baltimore won the next four games and its third world championship. "We have

"Iron man" Cal Ripken Jr. played in 19 straight All-Star Games during his 21-year career.

CAL RIPKEN JR.

always relied on our pitchers," noted catcher Rick Dempsey. "When you can roll out guys like Palmer, Flanagan, and McGregor every day, you're going to win a lot of games."

The team went through a gradual decline during the rest of the 1980s, however. Although stars such as Murray and Ripken continued to excel, the team's stellar pitching staff began to fall apart. By 1988, Palmer, Flanagan, McGregor, and both Dennis and Tippy Martinez were all gone. Without them, the Orioles suffered a major-league-record 21 straight losses at the start of the 1988 season.

{"IRON CAL"} The Orioles' sluggish performance continued into the early 1990s. Despite strong performances from Ripken and such newcomers as outfielder Brady Anderson and pitcher Mike Mussina, Baltimore continued to hover around the .500 mark. In 1992, the team moved from Memorial Stadium into Oriole Park at Camden Yards. Seemingly inspired by the new facility, the team responded with two straight winning seasons.

In 1994, the Orioles added slugging first baseman Rafael Palmeiro and were in a title chase until a players' strike ended the season. The following year, the team took a step backward with a

> The greatest Orioles pitcher since Jim Palmer, Mike Mussina led the league with 19 wins in **1995**.

MIKE MUSSINA

third-place finish, but on the night of September 6, baseball fans were treated to a special moment. That night, Cal Ripken Jr. was playing in his 2,131st consecutive game, breaking the major-league record set in 1939 by Yankees first baseman Lou "Iron Horse" Gehrig. With the game stopped, Ripken gave a speech and then jogged around the stadium, shaking hands with the cheering Baltimore fans.

*Left-hander Randy Myers came out of the bullpen to save 45 games for Baltimore in **1997**.*

"It's the least I could do," said Ripken. "Those fans have been with me every step of the way."

Ripken's streak continued until September 20, 1998, when he asked out of the lineup for the first time in 16 years. The streak of 2,632 consecutive games played stands as one of baseball's most hallowed records—one that may never be broken.

Driven by the great play of Ripken, Palmeiro, Anderson, and standout second baseman Roberto Alomar, the Orioles powered their

RANDY MYERS

way to the ALCS in both 1996 and 1997. Unfortunately, Baltimore came up short both times, losing to the New York Yankees and Cleveland Indians in five and six games, respectively.

{ BUILDING A WINNER THE ORIOLE WAY }

After 1997, the Orioles' fortunes dipped. The organization had gotten away from its formula of developing its own players through its minor-league system and had gotten into the expensive habit of signing free agents to shore up weak areas. Although the signings did produce playoff teams in 1996 and 1997, the strategy left the team with a huge payroll and no young impact players.

Still, there were individual highlights in the late '90s. Ripken belted his 400th home run in 1999 and notched his 3,000th hit in 2000, making him one of only seven major-leaguers to reach both milestones. At the beginning of the 2001 season, Ripken announced

From **1995** to **1998**, first baseman Rafael Palmeiro topped the 100-RBI mark every season.

RAFAEL PALMEIRO

A great fastball pitcher, 6-foot-6 Jason Johnson led a solid Baltimore pitching staff.

JASON JOHNSON

Tony Batista provided much-needed offensive pop in **2001**, smacking 25 home runs.

TONY BATISTA

that his 21st season would be his last. "Cal's retirement brings an end to one of the finest, most noble careers this game has ever seen," said fellow Orioles great Brooks Robinson.

As they started a new millennium, the Orioles looked to younger talents such as outfielder Chris Richard, third baseman Tony Batista, and pitchers Jason Johnson and Sidney Ponson to become the next generation of Orioles stars. With their development, the team hoped to return to its usual place among baseball's elite.

For nearly 50 years, the Baltimore Orioles have provided their fans with countless memories and championship excitement. Many of the finest players in the history of baseball have worn the orange and black colors of this proud franchise. For a city and a team with such long and glorious pasts, there can be no doubt that an equally bright future lies just beyond the horizon.

Lightning-quick second baseman Jerry Hairston Jr. looked to become a top leadoff hitter.

JERRY HAIRSTON JR.

NORTH CHICAGO
PUBLIC LIBRARY